HEINEMANN EDUCATIONAL BOOKS NIGERIA PLC
1 Ighodaro Road, Jericho, P.M.B. 5205, Ibadan
Phone: 417060 & 417061 *Telex:* 31113 HEBOOKS NG
Cable: HEBOOK Ibadan

Area Offices and Branches
Abeokuta . Akure . Bauchi . Benin City . Calabar . Enugu . Ibadan
Ikeja . Ilorin . Jos . Kano . Katsina . Maiduguri . Makurdi . Minna
Owerri . Port Harcourt . Sokoto . Uyo . Yola . Zaria

© Femi Osofisan 1991
First published 1991

ISBN 978-129-179-6

Printed and bound in Nigeria by
Johnmof Printers, Ibadan

Dedication

To
the memory of
duro ladipo

& for
biodun jeyifo:
even if the answers are not always as
simple;
& our choice is
- between cowards &
quixottes -
often painfully thin . . .

This play was first performed at the Arts Theatre, University of Ibadan, Nigeria from March 26 to March 30 1979, in a bilateral production by Sunbo Marinho and Funmi Dominu, with members of the Production Workshop of the Diploma Two (1978) of the Department of Theatre Arts. It was directed by the playwright himself, and had the following cast:

CAST

Robbers

ANGOLA	Demola Adeyemi
MAJOR	Tunji Oyelana
HASAN	Femi Osofisan
ALHAJA	Irene Orubo
AAFA	Femi Fatoba

Soldiers

SERGEANT	Gbade Sanda
CORPORAL	Kola Thomas
SOLDIER 1	John Oyarukua
SOLDIER 2	Ade Williams
SOLDIER 3	Humphrey Ojeifo
SOLDIER 4	Callistus Okoye
SOLDIER 5	Francis Evovo

Market Women

MAMA ALICE	**Bimbo Williams**
MAMA TOUN	**Gbemi Uddin**
MAMAL UYI	**Clementina Abone**
BINTU	**Tayo Omoniyi**
YEDUNNI	**Gladys Ekpiken**
BABY	**Didi Odigie**
DORA	**Remi Ogunsile**
ANGELINA	**Amatu Braide**

Traders Customers

James Osabuohien
Steve Waidor
Andrew Offeh
Tunde Laniyan
Ayo Akinwale

(This set and lights were designed by Sunbo Marinho, and music was by Tunji Oyelana.)

PROGRAMME NOTES TO THE FIRST PRODUCTION
(Full Text)

The phenomenon of armed robbery seems to me an apt metaphor of our age. But its reality outside the stage is of course far more brutal, devoid of any romanticism. With all our decrees and edicts, we have not succeed in taming this singular aspect of the violence of the age. And the problem has grown intractable, worsening with each passing day.

I believe that it is time we took a second look. The legalised slaughtering of the erring members of our society for whatever offence will certainly not bring the restoration of our society to its primodial sanity. Take a look at our salary structures, at the minimum wage level, count the sparse number of lucky ones who even earn it . . . and then take a look at the squalid spending habits of our egregious 'contractors' land speculators, middle men of all sorts, importers, exporters etc. Or take a look at our sprawling slums and ghettoes, our congested hospitals and crowded schools, our impossible markets . . . and then take another look at the fast proliferation of motor-cars, insurance agencies, supermarkets, chemist shops, boutiques, discotheques etc. The callous contradictions of our oil-doomed fantasies of rapid modernization.

It is obvious that as long as a single, daring nocturnal trip with a gun or matchet can yield the equivalent of one man's annual income, we shall continue to manufacture our own potential assassins. For armed robberies, on the scale we are witnessing, are the product of our unjust society.

Slogans about "returning to the land", sermons of bourgeois morality, are empty words to a man who is born condemned to poverty. Nor will public executions resolve the potency of oppression. The Bar Beach means death and disgrace, but so also does hunger, with a lingering certainty.

I hope this play shocks us into a new awareness. I hope it helps to change our attitude from passive acceptance or sterile indignation into a more dynamic, more enraged determination to confront ourselves and our lives. Else the four robbers will continue to rule our streets.

Prologue

(Lights begin to fall off in the auditorium, gradually leaving behind a pool of light which should be suggestive of moonlight. Commanding this spotlight is the STORY-TELLER, with a set of castanets or a sekere. He shouts out the traditional introductory formula: ALO O! As usual everybody replies: AAALO! He repeats this, get the same response, and playing his instrument, starts his song. The audience picks up the simple refrain - ALUGBINRIN GBINRIN! after each line. As the song gathers momentum, the musicians and the actors, hitherto lost within audience, begin to assemble on the stage.)

SONG OF THE STORY-TELLER [*]

> Iton mi dori o dori
> O dori dori
> Dori olosa merin o
> Danondanon akoni ni won
> Ajijofe apanilekun
> Awodi jeun epe
> Arinko sole dahoro
> Ron ni sorun apapandodo!
>
> Iton mi dori dori
> Dori olosa merin o
> Lojo ino ijoba jo won
> Owo boga gbogbo jaguda
> Ijoba wa kehin re sokun
> Iku egbere seriya oro
> Seriya iku ni won da fun

---

[*]   For English rendition of this song, as well as of others in the play, see the GLOSSARY at the end of the play text.

Seriya ota ibon
Kibon Kibon titibon-n-bon
Ha! eniyan kuku ewure
O wa dorun apapandodo!
Iton mi dori o dori
Dori olosa merin o
Ti won pade mi lojo kan
Ojo kan, olojo nkajo
Won ni: "Aafa a bewu yetu!
Yetu-yetu!
Eleni, yetu yetu!
Birugbon, yetu yetu!

Ah, jowo gba wa lowo won,
Eniyan araye titun
Owo nini o jewon a kobira
Owo nini o, owo yepere
Owo nini, ika sise,
Ika sise fi kole agbara
Ile kiko, ile yanturu
Gbanilaya, wa faye su ni
Daniloro fagbara ko ni"

Iton mi dori o dori
Dori olosa merin o
Danondanon akoni ni won
Ajijofe apanilekun
Awodi jeun epe

Awodi jeun epe
Arinko sole dahoro
Ran ni sorun apapandodo
Ran ni sorun apapandodo

2

(Already the actors and musicians have gathered on the stage, evidently all in a light mood, as they recognize one another and exchange warm greetings. Then, discovering the costumes, they begin to pick and choose, and then to dress up, gradually establishing the various roles they will be playing. The STORYTELLER, still chanting, joins them, and is promptly offered a long flowing buba in white, a mat and a small kettle. He shrugs and accepts, and the song ends in a slow fade out. Almost immediately afterwards the lights begin to return, and we are in - PART ONE . . .)

PART ONE

(A market in a small town, with stalls and various items. The time is dawn. Centre-stage is a set of barrels, arranged one upon another behind a tall white stake. Now people begin to gather in various groups in the half light. Soldiers lead in a prisoner and tie him to the stake. Then, at the orders of their officer, they take position. They fire. The prisoners slumps. A doctor steps forward to examine the body. The soldiers untie the corpse and carry it out. One by one, the crowd drifts out after the soldiers in the direction of town. The entire scene is mute, except for the military march which starts before the coming of lights and fades out with the departure of the soldiers. As lights slowly increase now with the growing day, a cock crows, and we notice that a group of four — a woman and three men — has stayed behind, watching the departing crowd. The woman, who is AL-HAJA, is sobbing and soon collapses. MAJOR turns and goes to her. She begins a slow dirge:)

ALHAJA

(singing) Eni lo sorun kii bo
Alani o digbere, o darinnoko o

Eni lo sorun, aremabo o
Alani o digbere, o doju ala o!
Ohun won nje lorun ni o bawon je,
Ma jokun, ma jekolo o,
Alani o digbere, o darinnoko o...

(HASAN and ANGOLA are also standing by her now, the latter still shaking with fury.)

4

ANGOLA

What do you think they'll do with his body?

HASAN

Eat it, the cannibals. Share the meat among their wives and children.

ALHAJA

(sobbing) My husband!

ANGOLA

Like a ram. They slaughtered our leader like a ramadan lamb.

HASAN

Or worse. With that cloth tied over his face, they denied him even the privilege of bleating.

ANGOLA

They must pay for this.

HASAN

(rising) They will pay. They or their children.

ALHAJA

My poor husband.

MAJOR

Let's go, Alhaja. I told you not to come.

HASAN

It was disgusting. Five o'clock in the morning, as cold as in harmattan, yet they all came out to watch, to gloat over his death.

ANGOLA

And their faces, did you see that? None of them flinched
even once at the crack of the guns. They were so eager to
devour him.

HASAN

Like vultures

ANGOLA

Like hounds.

HASAN

Each one went away with a piece of his flesh.
Enough to last a month's feast of gossiping.

ANGOLA

I know the sergeant. His wife sells at that stall over there.
It won't be difficult to get him.

MAJOR

Let's go now Alhaja. I'll see you home.

ANGOLA

Leave her alone, abi!

MAJOR

The morning's rising.

HASAN

Let it rise. We've got a wound to avenge.

MAJOR

No. Not any more.

ANGOLA

What do you mean? I say what do you mean?

MAJOR

Are you all so blind then that you can't see the truth?

MAJOR

It's finished, finished. We've come to the end of the road.

ANGOLA

What! What's that rubbish from your mouth?

MAJOR

The only rubbish I know is you standing there, you bundle of guinea-worm . . .

ANGOLA

By Allah, I'll . . .

HASAN

(interposing) No!

ANGOLA

Let me mangle the foul-mouthed coward.

MAJOR

Coward! Is your grandfather present then?

ANGOLA

You hear him!

HASAN

I say wait. Let him explain.

ANGOLA

What does he have to explain? A chicken, that's what he's always been. Even when the Leader was alive.

MAJOR

Raise your voice now. Other people are here to save you from harm. The dog boasts in town, but everybody knows the tiger's in the bush.

ALHAJA

(who has been looking at them in horror) Oh my poor husband. They've taken his body away, and all you can do is fight among yourselves! I'm going away! I'm going after them.

MAJOR

Hold it, Alhaja. Listen to me, if only for the last time. The party's over and it's going to be every man for himself from now on.

ANGOLA

You hear!

MAJOR

Face the truth man! Ever since this new decree on armed robbery, * we've been finished! You can only walk that far on the edge of a blade. Sooner or later, the blade cuts in.

ANGOLA

And so you'll run, isn't it? Like a cheap half-kobo pickpocket in the market pursued by women. You think -

ANGOLA

(taking out his knife) One more step, Angola and your blood's going to wet this market. You think because you have the brain of an ox, everybody's got to be as dumb? They've got the Leader, what more is left?

HASAN

We are left. We'll fight them.

MAJOR

Till the last man! Well, good luck to you.
I am off. I want to live.

ANGOLA

Only if we let you, don't forget. No one deserts and lives.

MAJOR

As in the joke book, eh? *(laughs.)* There's none of you that can stop me now the leader's dead. Either singly or all together. You can try. *(They form a ring round him. He*

---

* The Federal Military Government of Nigeria under General Gowon passed a decree making armed robbery punishable by public execution. The gruesome practice only ended with the coming of a civilian administration in 1979.

waits.) No one moves. Alhaja, let's go.

HASAN

You've always been a friend, Major. Even if I wanted, I could never raise my knife against you. But what's this you're doing? With an oath, we bound our lives together —

MAJOR

Yes. Our lives, not our corpses.

ANGOLA

Listen to him! It's disgusting! What are you if not a corpse? Tell me. You were born in the slum and you didn't know you were a corpse? Since you burst out from the womb, all covered in slime, you've always been a corpse. You fed on worms and left-overs, your body nude like a carcasse in the government mortuary, elbowing your way among other corpses. And the stink is all over you like a flodded cemetery in Lagos . . .

MAJOR

I'll be a living corpse then! Our Leader swore the whole army could not subdue him. He is dead now.

ANGOLA

Yes, but he died! The decree smashed him.
(Alhaja is singing the dirge. They pause and watch her, Hasan smoking.)

ANGOLA

And he died bravely.

MAJOR

Yes, but he died! The decree smashed him.
*Alhaja is singing the dirge. They pause and watch her,
Hasan smoking.)*

ANGOLA

Don't go with him, Alhaja. He's on their side you can see.
The Leader always suspected it too. Every time we went
on a raid and had to kill, he broke down and sobbed like a
silly school pickin.

MAJOR

Life is life, and human life's still valuable.

ANGOLA

Pele o, alufa!* Only you never failed to collect your share
of the loot.

MAJOR

Because I always did my share. And more, whatever the
personal cost! On that famour raid on the UAC store at
Mapo, who was it that silenced the guards? Three of them,
and single-handed! And when the Police drove in with
their guns and dogs, was it not me who covered the rear
while you escaped with the goods? And the trip to the cus-
toms shed at Ikeja, who planned it? Who tore that crazy
captain off the locks of the gate in defiance of the
electrified wires? Who slipped back afterwards to set the
place on fire so as to cover our tracks? And others. And
more . . .

---

* Literally, 'Thank you, moralizing priest!'

HASAN

Yes, go on, Major! Omo jaguda!* Sleek snake of the underworld!

MAJOR

(Pleased, starts song, which they all join:)
Awa ti wa a o ko, a o ko
Sasangbaku wosi wosi

A belemu memu
A belelubo jelubo
Kako won nisu
Samusamu la mu
Gbegede de ge
Sasara lobe
Danfo la duro!

MAJOR

(exultant) — That Alhaji in Kano with his ten Alsatians and fifty guards! That night, when his lorries of contraband arrived from Maradi! Have you forgotten their faces when I rose up from among the bales of lace cloth, two machine guns under my armpit! *(HASAN is on knees, pleading desperately for mercy.)* Ha ha ha! The Police sing my name in sixteen state! . . .

HASAN

(singing and stamping his foot. Major joins:)
Bi e ba gbo giri, e sa o!
Awa la ro giri, kile ya!
Bi a ba de giri, e sa o!
Awa la ro giri, kile ya!
_____
*   Son of a robber!'

12

Awa la ro giri, kile ya! -

MAJOR

(breaking off) But alas it's finished. I knew it that day we failed to rescue the Leader from prison. *(Alhaja starts to dirge softly, he faces her.)* Sing on, Alhaja, sing on, but we shall not mourn! Tears are useless, they screen off the truth of sight. We built a world, and they tore it down. Think, that night! The lives wasted, the blood spilt. How many men did we lose, how many of us left now of a whole army of warriors?

HASAN

(sad) Just the four of us, but sti"! —

MAJOR

Four! The others slaughtered, fine, fine men, the best . . . Sarumi, the leader of the coast, who knew the creeks like the back of his palm —

HASAN

He handled boats like cradling a child —

MAJOR

His ringing laugh! When he cunningly led officers on his trail to quicksand and watched them flounder like *agbegijo* . . . Poor fish of the creeks, you had no feet deft enough for land. As he scaled the prison walls that night by my side, the police bullets ripped his flesh. I can still hear his dying scream . . . And Agala —

---

* agbegijo: traditional Yoruba masquarader/acrobat.

HASAN

The darling of the Lebanese —

MAJOR

Yes, of those white-skinned Ogboni* of Gbagi. He understood too well their weakness for young rounded black flesh, and had an army of women at his command. Oh! he never failed to know weeks in advance of coming consignments, especially those arriving through the numerous underground channels which the Labanese control —

ALHAJA

He too, they cut him down that night as he ran forward with the explosives. The blast took him and his men.

MAJOR

Lamilami, the eternal husband of the women of Jankara** —

HASAN

Ebiti, his assistant at Oyingbo**, who tried to branch out to Sapon**.

HASAN

Till the women found out that his main supply was a unique strain of Gonorrhea — *(They laugh)*

ALHAJA

The bullets have cured that now. He went with the others --

---

*   Ogboni: A feared, secret cult among the Yoruba.
**   Jankara, Oyingbo, Sapon: famous markets
*** Mushin, a Lagos suburb, overpopulated and crime-infested.

14

MAJOR

Sir Love, De Niger Nigger —

HASAN

The best car thieves of the century, who could drive a car non-stop from Mushin to the Cameroun border, sell it--

MAJOR

And steal it back again to sell to young officers ambitious for rapid promotions! Shall I go on? Sago? Bente? Mada? who could pick the lock of any house with their teeth!

ALHAJA

All, all mown down in one single night.

(The mourning mood returns. MAJOR starts singing a funeral tribute which they all join. He breaks off.)

MAJOR

Listen, Angola, Hasan, Alhaja! Listen to me, this is the end. The guns will get us too in our turn, unless we quit.

HASAN

But for what? Where do we go?

ALHAJA

Nowhere. They've trapped us with their guns and decrees.

HASAN

All we have left is the Bar Beach.* And then six feet in the ground.

---

* the Bar Beach of Lagos: the most notorious venue at the time for the public execution of robbers.

ALHAJA

    (sings a dirge:)
    O se kere-e-e-e
    O se kere e-e-e
    O se kere eye ora
    Eye ora ti nfori so
    Arugbo n sunkun a fi so fa
    A fi sofa a fi ya loge
    Aloge yo gongo laya
    O se kere-e-e
    O se kere-e-e ...

MAJOR

    But perhaps? ... If we tried ... somewhere ...? *(Alhaja is still singing. But suddenly, over her voice, rises another song, from behind one of the stalls. They start, and then instinctively dash for cover, Major dragging Alhaja with him. The STORY TELLER, as AAFA now, emerges with a ma and a small kettle.)*

AAFA

    (singing as he spreads the mat:)

    Ataiyatu: lilahi
    Azakiyatu: lilahi
    Ike Oluwa lilahi
    Ige Oluwa lilahi
    Ko lo ba Mohamadu: lilahi
    Ataiyatu Salamatu: lilahi!

    (He starts to wash his his hands and feet preparatory to sta ing his prayer. ANGOLA and HASAN are crawling towar him stealthily, but he feigns not to notice. But as they rai

their hands to grab him, he shouts:)

AAFA

Robi najhini wahaali mimo yahamalum![*]

(ANGOLA and HASAN swivel towards each other instead and begin to embrace, grinning sheepishly).

AAFA

(without looking at them or interrupting his ablutions) Haba! will you lay your filthy hands upon the servant of Allah? Walahu hairu hafizan, wauwa arihamu rohimin!^{**}

(ANGOLA and HASAN separate and begin to slap each other methodically, bowing politely each time and seeming to enjoy the pain)

AAFA

(looking at them) — The bat has no eyes, but jt roams with ease in the dark. They think chameleon is a dandy, but if he were to talk what strategies of dissimulation he'd teach our cleverest spies *(seems to calm down)* Bisimilahi ar-rahmani rahim!^{***} Sit down, it is time for prayers.

(ANGOLA and HASAN cease their fighting and take praying postures. They begin to knock their foreheads on the mat in a slowly growing rhythm. AAFA who has shut his eyes, suddenly cries out:)

17

AAFA

Come out, you two! Come out!

(ALHAJA and MAJOR creep out)

ALHAJA

(hesitantly) Sallu ala nabiyyi karim!*

AAFA

(grudgingly) Salla lahu alayhi wasalam**. I see you have been able to pick up a few things from your lovers.

ALHAJA

Whoever you are —

AAFA

Join us. It is time for prayers.

MAJOR

Aafa, whoever you are, we meant you no harm —

AAFA

No, only to rob me.

MAJOR

It was a mistake, Allah! We don't steal from men of God —

AAFA

You only cut their throat.

---

*   Pray for the Noble Prophet!
**   God grant him blessings and peace!

ALHAJA

I swear to you Aafa! One death s enough for the morning. We supplied the corpse.

AAFA

Alihamidu lilai. Your husband, was it? *ALHAJA and MAJOR are started. He chuckles).* Alhaja! Yes, I recognize you. At the war-front, when you traded across the lines, selling to both sides, it was convenient then, wasn't it, to call yourself Alhaja? But your longest pilgrimage as we all know was to the officers' beds, not to Mecca!

ALHAJA

(furious) And so what, you disgusting old man! I survived didn't I? And what do you think matters beyond that? I survived, but I don't go raking up muck like a municipal waste disposal van. Spill it out then, since you are a refuse depot, let's hear the rest of the rubbish!

MAJOR

(trying to restrain her) Alhaja ... Alhaja ...

ALHAJA

No! I am not scared of him! No one trifles with me, even on a day like this, and gets away with it! A pebble sits light in a catapult, but it still squashes the lizard! Let him take care!

AAFA

Leave her. Truth is a bitter thing. I suppose you take me for a leather merchant.

ALHAJA

Release these men from your diabolical spell!

AAFA

Not me, but Allah, whose ways are mysterious. He has chosen to reclaim these lost souls for his service. Who are we to intervene? See, their zeal is an example even to the devout.

MAJOR

Old man, we don't know you. We've done you no harm. Or are you from the Police?

AAFA

I am not concerned about the Police.
Grey hair, they say, is of age.

MAJOR

I understand, Aafa. We're sorry.

ALHAJA

I am not!

MAJOR

Aafa, nobody quarrels so much with his head that he wears his hat on his knees.

AAFA

Allah akbar! Grey hair is not sold in the market. When fools mistake a beard for the mustache of impertinence, then they must pay the penalty.

MAJOR

Forgive us. It's hunger that drives us.

AAFA

As it drives other people. But not into crime.

ALHAJA

(angrily) You mean, not publicly.

MAJOR

We are honest. We steal only from the rich.

AAFA

Foolish! *(Gestures)* Get up you two, Allah is not likely to hear your prayers. Fools, all of you. You steal from the rich, so where will you hide? The rich are powerful.

MAJOR

Yes, we know.

AAFA

Where will you run? They make the laws.

MAJOR

Yes, and they build the law courts.

HASAN

Train the lawyers.

ANGOLA

They own the firing squads. *(sings)* O se kere-e- e-e . . .

AAFA

So why not give up? There's enough employment in the country.

MAJOR

Yes. The rich also own the servants.

AAFA

And you cannot be servants? You? You? (*Looks at them in turn*) And you self-styled Alhaja? (*The robbers laugh heartily.*)

ALHAJA

(*in 'illiterate' accent*) 'Wanted urgently: Four boy and a one girls. Standard Six an adfantage but not compulsory—Position—

HASAN

(*same game*) 'Service Boys. Waiter! Attractive salary —

MAJOR

'Five naira per week!

ALHAJA

(*reading off AAFA's bald head*) 'Vacancy. Fast-growing company. Excellent opportunities for ambitious young men willing to work with their hands. Position-

ANGOLA

'Cleaner!'

HASAN

'Cook!'

ALHAJA

'Housemaid, part-time mistress!.

MAJOR

'Washerman!'

ANGOLA

Like dogs. To lap up the excrement.

AAFA

Your pride! Is that it! The eloquent pride of the masses!
Will that feed you? Clothe you? Shelter your children?
Will it halt the bullets when your backs are tied to the
stake?

MAJOR

(jeering, starts the song:)

O ja lori obi
O ja lori obi o fiton se
E so faya wo!
Eni ba rohun tafala ti o mu
Eni ba rohun taraka ti o gbe o
Sonitohun yode, sohun mi siwin
Sonitohun dope, sohun mi rago!
Kerikeri! Kerikeri!
Bi we ti mbo kode i pa e loru?
Omugo jaguda lode ma i pa
Jaguda ni won pe wa
Sugbon awa mà mo pe ise la nse!
Eni Esu ba ron lowo, ko deno de wa
Eni ba fe ku, ko ni bo lawa ma gba?
Ifun alayen, ni gbangba ni o ba!
Edo oniyen, ni gbangba ni o ba!

ANGOLA

Right, Aafa, so the journey ends. At the Bar Beach, in some market place, at the outskirts of town. What does it matter? For those not in the privileged position to steal government files, award contracts—

HASAN

Alter accounts —

ANGOLA

Swear affidavits —

ALHAJA

Grant sick leaves —

HASAN

Sell contraband —

MAJOR

Collude with aliens* —

ANGOLA

And buy chieftaincy titles as life insurance! No, let our obituaries litter the public places and one day —

AAFA

What illusions!

(They assault. AAFA suddenly, led by ALHAJA who deliberately and obscenely violates the startled man. They are singing in chorus, with HASAN taking the solo:)

---

* In production, the list should be made to include the most recent public scandals.

Eyi lo ye ni
Hen hun hen!
Eyi lo ye ni
Hen hun hen!
Ogun lo nrogun
Hen hun hen
Epon meje
Hen hun hen!
Okon fota
Hen hun hen!
Meji femu
Hen hun hen!
Merin fato!

(As AAFA retreats rather ungainly, the robbers collapse in laughter. But gradually AAFA himself is infected by their mirth. He smiles. Visibly his mood turns benign as he sits down among them.)

AAFA

Alright! I'll help you.

ANGOLA

We're no beggers!

AAFA

I said, help. I can make you rich.

HASAN

You?

MAJOR

How?

AAFA

I'll put a power in your hands that will take you out of the gutters. Into the most glittering palaces.

ALHAJA

Don't mock us, Aafa.

AAFA

Alhaja, we know each other, don't we? We can hardly afford children's games.

ALHAJA

Then talk.

AAFA

(smiling) You're a cunning one. You put on this cloth of earth and you think no one will recognize you.

ALHAJA

What do you mean?

AAFA

It will come out one day, I assure you. Maybe in violent conflict.

ALHAJA

I have known conflicts, old man. Look in the police records. Violence, I feed on it. Don't think you can frighten me.

MAJOR

But what's the man talking about? I thought you wanted to make us rich.

ANGOLA

He's beginning to dodge.

AAFA

She's deep. Deep. She has such reserves of power. For-
tunately the earth has folded her in its skin

ANGOLA

Let us go.

MAJOR

Old man —

AAFA

Promise!

ANGOLA

(amidst the general exclamation) I beg your pardon?

AAFA

If you want to leave your poverty behind, on the dungheap
of this day, promise me.

MAJOR

We do not understand.

AAFA

Three promises, and you'll be on the highway to riches.

MAJOR

The first?

AAFA

Never to rob the poor.

ANGOLA

But we've just told you —

AAFA

Promise! *(holds out his 'tira')* I know the poor, they do not love each other.

MAJOR

*(licking the 'tira')*Promised. *(They do so in turn.)*

ANGOLA

And the second promise?

AAFA

To rob only the public places. Not to choose your victims as you do among solitary women. Not to break into homes.

MAJOR

Alright! promised! *(Again the ritual of assent)*

HASAN

Now let's hear the third.

AAFA

The most important. You must promise never again to take a human life.

ANGOLA

No, Aafa, too many objections. First, one Sergeant owes us a debt. Then there are many citizens who must be made to account for their wealth, and the poverty of their workers. Such accounts can be settled only one way.

HASAN

And what of our protection? If one of the victims recognizes us in the course of an operation, shall we let him go?

AAFA

It's a risk you must take

HASAN

And the Sergeant?

AAFA

He also goes free. And aş for the·others, you will have to allow the country to settle its own accounts. On these conditions alone will I give you my help, If you still want to be ːich. Do you promise or shall I go on my way?

MAJOR

Yes, promised! *(They do so again, all but ANGOLA.)*

ANGOLA

Aafa, too many poeple ride their cars along the sore-ridden backs of the poor. Is there no other way?

AAFA

None, son. Otherwise it'll be an empty force in your hands. I do not control it.

MAJOR

Promise, Angola. Let's first have the power.

AAFA

It's not a power you can cheat, I warn you. It makes its own laws.

ANGOLA

(after much prodding from others) — Alright, I promise.

AAFA

The last thing I want to tell you is that you can use this power only three times. Three times. After that it dies. But if you use it well, even once is sufficient to make you rich.

HASAN

Don't worry, Aafa. We need just enough to be able to organize ourselves again.

AAFA

Well, it's just that you never can tell about human greed. And because of that, I am going to teach each of you only one part of the formula, so none can cheat the others. No, no, don't protest, I have a knowledge of human beings. The power will work only if all of you combine and each speaks his verse, in his own voice. Now, take, one for each of you. *(He distributes four seeds.)* Swallow it. *(From the folds of his buba, he brings out an opele* *The robbers are surprised.)* Ah, if only one way led to the stream, how many women would fill their pots? Just say after me now: *(He chants the following verse, the robbers repeating antiphonally the lines:)*

---

* opele: divination chain used by priests of Ifa.

Omo Enire
Omo Enire
Omo enikan saka bi agbon
Ifa ka rele o
Ewi nle Ado
Onsa n'Deta
Erinmi lode Owo
Ifa ka rele o
Gbolajokoo, omo okinkin
Tii meriin fon
Ifa ka rele o
Omo opolopo imo
Tii tu jijia wodo
Omo asese yo ogomo
Tii fun nigin nigin
Omo ejo meji
Tii sare ganranganran lori irawe
Omo ina joko mo jeeluju
Ifa ka rele o

That's it! All that remains now is for you to sing —

ALL

Sing!

AAFA

Yes, sing and dance. It's an irresistible power.
Once you begin to sing, anyone within hearing distance
stops whatever he is doing and joins. He will sing and
dance and then head for his home to sleep. And he won't
wake till the next morning.

HASAN

(suspicious) — You're not pulling our leg, Aafa?

AAFA

Haba! You're so hard to please. I've given you so much power for free! No more fear of the Bar Beach if you keep the injunctions. Robbery, but without violence —

MAJOR

Aafa, don't mind us. It's just that it's all so . . . so bewildering . . .

AAFA

I know it is. But if you don't want to try it —

MAJOR

Of course we do! We've nothing else anyway.

AAFA

Right, it's a lot, and I don't want it wasted. If you're sure of using it, I'll teach you the opening formula now . . . but, look I can see the women coming, let's leave this place.

(*They go out hastily. The market women begin to arrive now, in groups or singly. The usual greetings, and then the bustle opening the stalls, setting out the wares. The goods are the usual items of the West African market: foodstuff, bales of cloth, clothes, utensils, portable electronic equipment, etc., items that should generally be easy to clear from the stage. The conversations focus mainly on the execution of that morning, and the expected relief from robbers for some time. Then suddenly, from off-stage, the first strains of music approaching. The robbers are singing:*)

Ewe a je	Herbs will answer!
Oosa a je	gods will respond!
Ewe a je	Herbs will answer!
Oosa a je	gods will respond!
E-e-e!	E-e-e!
Boo gbaso wa oja	If you have come to market with cloth
Maa jo, etc.	Dance!
Boo gbesu wa oja	If with yams, Dance! etc . . .

Other items of the market are mentioned in the song. As the song grows louder, ever before the robbers appear on stage, the traders and clients, in very abrupt transitions, join the song and begin to dance. The robbers dance in. The scene recalls a carnival. One by one, in small groups, the market people dance out, leaving the robbers who soon fall down laughing.)

MAJOR

It worked! Ah, it worked!

HASAN

God, what a harvest!

ANGOLA

I can't believe it!

ALHAJA

Get up, you fools. Let's start packing, it's going to take the whole day.

(They begin to assemble the items into convenient packs, singing and dancing. Lights fade slowly into a BLACK-OUT.)

INTERLUDE

(As the stage is prepared for the next scene, the AAFA appears in a spotlight, singing and dancing. As before the refrain is sung by actors, stage-hands and audience. The AAFA sings:

Iton mi dori o dori
Dori olosa merin o
Mo wa fun won lagbara
Agbara orin kiko
Orin kiko ijo jijo
Ijo jijo fi kun won lorun
Emi Aafa a bewu yetu!
Yetu-yetu!
Eleni, yetu yetu!
Birugbon, yetu yetu!
Ologbon, yetu yetu!

Bee mo setutu fun won
Nitori araye titun
Owo nini o jewon o kobira
Owo nini, ika sise
Ika sise fi kole agbara
Ile kiko, ile yanturu
Gbanilaya, wa faye su ni
Daniloro fagbara koni

Iton mi dori o dori
Dori olosa merin o
Danondanon akoni no won
Ajijofe apanilekun

34

Awodi jeun epe
Arinko sole dahoro
Ron ni sonun a sunlo fonfon . . .

(The lights slowly fade out.)

PART TWO

(Same market' about a fortnight later. Late afternoon going into evening. The market obviously in its dying moments: stall are being shut, boxes arranged, accounts added. People are chanting and singing, and there is a general air of satisfaction. Fully visible are some soldiers on guard. The Sergeant, going around, finally stops by the stall of MAMA ALICE, leader of the market women).

SERGEANT

Well, Mama Alice, good sales today?

MAMA ALICE

Extraordinary, Sergeant. In all my days of trading, I can't recollect another day like this. And I can see, looking round, that it's the same for everybody. It's a pity your wife chose today of all days to be ill. *(Giving him stool.)* Sit?

SERGEANT

I'm thirsty.

MAMA ALICE

As always! You don't have to announce it.

SERGEANT

You and the others made great profits today, but it's because we've been on our feet all day.

MAMA ALICE

Oh I'm grateful, but the day I see you otherwise than thirsty— *(calls)* Bintu, any wine left or is it all gone?

BINTU

No, one keg left, but it's the only one. Sale's been fantastic today.

MAMA ALICE

Bring it, I'll buy the last one.

BINTU

(Coming with the keg, seeing the Sergeant:) If it's for Baba Mayo —

MAMA ALICE

Who else do you think?

BINTU

I knew it just had to be him!

SERGEANT

Listen, you women —

BINTU

Sergeant, today's my lucky day, you can have the wine free. You and your men have been wonderful.

MAMA ALICE

Yes, Bintu, call the other soldiers to share the wine, I don't think Sergeant will mind. They all deserve our gratitude.

SERGEANT

Yes, they can leave their posts now. The sun's falling anyway.

(Bintu goes to call the soldeirs)

MAMA ALICE

You're right. We're already packing up. Our problem is going to be how to carry our profits home. Some of us will used porters!

SERGEANT

I'm glad. I need a promotion.

MAMA ALICE

If they ask for a recommendation, come to me. All the market women will sign for you. Ah, the goddess of the market woke with us today. Right from dawn the customers came pouring in.

SERGEANT

What do you expect, after two weeks of shutting the market?

MAMA ALICE

What we lost in that last raid! I tell you, if the government hadn't given us protection, none of us would have come back.

(The other soldiers join. Mama Alice and Bintu pour out the wine for them. The Sergeant waves aside the salutes and lights his pipe.)

SERGEANT

Well . . . your friends didn't come today

MAMA ALICE

No, thanks to you. And they are not my friends.

SERGEANT

(*laughing*) Alright, no need to take offence. You see, our guns were so cocked and alert that, had we hear so much as a humming, the market would have been littered with corpses. Ask these brutes!

(*General laughter. More women, prepared for home, join the group from time to time.*)

CORPORAL

Ah, you should have seen me, Serg! Once, when I thought I heard a song-(*He leaps forward suddenly, grabs one of his mates by the neck, forcing him down with a "gun" to his ribs. They begin to play-act:*)

CORPORAL

Caught you, you scoundrel-

SOLDIER

(*stammering with fear*) So-so-so . . . ja! Soja!

CORPORAL

'Do-re-mi', is it? I will 'do-re-mi' you with bullets today! Robber!

SOLDIER

Bu-u-u-ut, soja . . . !

CORPORAL

Quiet! You can't even sing a healthy, masculine song! 'Do-re-mi-fa-soh'! Disgusting! Are you one of these wall geckos from England?

SOLDIER

I'm telling you

CORPORAL

No! you want to sing, abi? You think that can work on a
soldier? There, sing now! I've got my palm across your
smelling mouth, and if you - yeah!

(Sudden scream. He rolls off clutching his fingers.)

SERGEANT

What happened. Corple?

CORPORAL

No respect for fair play, Serg. Teeth! He bit me!

SERGEANT -

Ah-ha, so did you arrest him?

CORPORAL

Serg, I couldn't

SERGEANT

He bit you again?

CORPORAL

No, Serg. It was my own uncle, Chief Okedoke. Oh the
kick he gave me afterwards . . .
*(More laughter. Some of the women retie their visibly bulging
wallets.)*

BINTU

He should have broken your head, I don't know why he

didn't!

MAMA ALICE

You see how they mock us.

MAMA TOUN

They don't believe we were robbed.

SERGEANT

By musicians! Tell us another.

MAMA ALICE

You know, I almost wish the robbers had returned today.

WOMEN

Ah, no-o! The gods forbid! Especially not today!

MAMA ALICE

No, I mean, if only to convince these men.

SOLDIER

I am convinced. And I can even make a few guesses. The robbers didn't turn up because last night, their leader developed a sore throat.

SOLDIER

No, no. It was the lead drum. It burst in rehearsal.

SOLDIER

They thought of a better method, I tell you. They are waxing the music on a disc, then they can rob the whole nation by playing it on the radio.

SOLDIER

The hit parade!

BINTU

You hear them! So the whole market was drunk or dreaming? And the goods lost?

(The Sergeant starts the song which the others take up and sing with great enthusiasm:)

ENI MAYE JE
Eni maye je
E e ni gungi agbon o
Eni fe kaye re o gun
E e ni gungi agbon se!
Bi ofun yun ni a o ronu iko
Bi ofun yun ni a ronu kele
Eni ba salejo fun Mus'limi
Se ohun logbejo salamulekum o!
Paga! bi gunungun ba lorule
Oro penuda, inowo poosi
Ohun buruku ma semi lalejo o,
Ng o ni reru gagagugu
Arun laa wo,
A ma i woku o!

(They collapse in laughter. Some women help Mama Alice to tidy her stall, etc . . .)

SERGEANT

Alright, so there was a robbery. But tell us, in earnest what really happened?

BINTU

How many times do you want us to repeat it? Suddenly
there was this song, from nowhere —

SOLDIER

From nowhere —

BINTU

It was so enchanting, so sweet —

SOLDIER

So sweet —

SOLDIER

Africa 70!

SOLDIER

Shut up, I'm beginning to hear it myself!

BINTU

It's the truth! Mama Toun here began to dance.

MAMA TOUN

Ah, it was Mama Uyi!

MAMA UYI

Me? I only followed Yedunni!

YEDUNNI

Liar! You danced first!

MAMA ALICE

We all danced. No one could resist the music.

SERGEANT

Ah, women!

MAMA ALICE

There were men in the market too. And they danced.

BINTU

I tell you no one could resist it. We sang and danced in a dink of dream.

CORPORAL

You sang too!

BINTU

We sang too!

BINTU

We were all possessed.

CORPORAL

And then you fell asleep

BINTU

When we woke —

SERGEANT

The next morning —

MAMA ALICE

Yes the next morning, can you believe that!

BINTU

And no one in the town even getting suspicious —

MAMA TOUN

Until the next morning!

BINTU

Too late, everything was gone, all we brought to sell.

SOLDIER

To where?

YEDUNNI

Why don't you tell us idiot! *(General laughter as the soldier pursues her.)*

MAMA ALICE

Well, my friends, night is falling fast and we must leave. But before we go, please let us show our gratitude to Baba Mayo and his men by singing them our market song.

(She starts, and they join, dancing and dancing.)

SONG OF THE MARKET

The work of profit
brought us to this world,
this life that is a market.
Some sell who come and flourish
and some ...
who pay their ... in gold!
...

Among the crowd
that's born each day,
just to sweep the rubbish,

45

and scour round like dogs,
count not our kins!
Let's not only stay
rambling around the market,
to eat discarded bits!

The lure of profit
has conquered our souls
and changed us into cannibals:
oh praise the selfless British
who with the joyous sound
of minted coins and gold
brought us civilization!

We make inflation
and hoard away
as much as we may relish
essential commodities
like sugar and salt
like milk and oil
so we can leave the market
each day a-rolling in wealth!

The lust of profit
keeps us in this world
this life that is a market:
refuse to join and perish,
rebel and quench!
For those who spit at gold,
otosi asinniwaye!
Among the few
that's seen each day
whipping the world with lashes

and strutting round like lords,
let's count our sons!
Let's also say
as we collect our profit
that life is heaven on earth!

SERGEANT

To be frank with you, I'm just dying to meet your musicians. I'm sure I could do with some exercise

MAMA ALICE

Apart from drinking, you mean. A dance will certainly do something to your pregnancy!

(They are still laughing when the first strains of the robbers' music float in. The music grows louder, approaching. With an oath, the Sergeant springs up, spilling his drink, and reaches for his gun. But it's too late, his movement ends unexpectedly in a dance posture. The women point at him and laugh, and before they know it, have started to dance and sing. The transition, as in the last scene must be very abrupt. Now the robbers come in as before, singing and drumming. They hasten among the traders to untie their wallets, search their bags and all places they suspect money will be, including inside their bras. The soldiers of course are not neglected in the search. Finally, on the last stanza of the song, the traders and the soldiers dance out. MAJOR follows them, but is not immediately noticed by the others.)

HASAN

(exultant) I told you didn't I? See how it worked!

ALHAJA

You're a genius, Hasan!

ANGOLA

So easy. No more tedious work like last time. Carrying off those heavy basket and boxes. Finding a place to hide them. Then looking for a market to sell them without being suspected.

HASAN

All that's gone. Now we just wait till they've finished the haggling and hustling and are ready to go home with the profits. Then we pounce.

ALHAJA

A tune and a song. And we rake a fortune.

ANGOLA

Look at this! Who would believe these women made so much even in one month!

HASAN

What I have here is going to need a basket to carry.

ANGOLA

And did you see the soldiers! They actually brought soldiers to catch us!

HASAN

Fools! Guns to catch a song!

ALHAJA

I particularly liked that Sergeant. It was a delight to watch his dance. *(Dances in imitation. They laughs, except Hasan.)*

HASAN

(pensive) Yes, the Sergeant. How time changes fast.

ALHAJA

What?

HASAN

Time changes all of us.

ANGOLA

You knew him?

HASAN

A corpse, that's what we all become in the end. Yes, I knew the Sergeant, intimately. But how he has changed!

ALHAJA

Lucky then that he didn't recognize you.

HASAN

A corpse! *(laughs suddenly).* Forget it, the death mark is on all of us, even if we never reach the bar Beach.

ANGOLA

Hasan, this is not time to be mournful.. Look at what you have in your hands.

HASAN

(listlessly) Money . . .

ANGOLA

A fortune! The Aafa was right. We didn't make much last time, having to sell through shady channels. But this time we've got enough to last many life-times of poverty.

ALHAJA

Let's go! I'm dying to count.

HASAN

Wait, where's Major?

MAJOR

(entering: he has one of the soldiers' guns) Here.

HASAN

What do you want with a —

MAJOR

Stop! Don't move any of you. *(kicks out a sack).* Alhaja, take this sack and collect all the money. You heard me! *(Reluctantly, she does so.)* And I warn you, no one else is to move. I love you all, but I won't hesitate to shoot any of you.

HASAN

(handing his share over to Alhaja) This is treachery.

MAJOR

Treachery?

HASAN

The money belongs to all of us.

MAJOR

Bring it to me, Alhaja. Slowly. *(takes it from her)* Thanks.
The money belongs to me now.

ALHAJA

(angry) My husband brought you out of the slum. From the
cold, he put clothes on your back. From the rain, he found
you shelter. He put your scattered life together, raised you
into a man. He put the first gun in your hand, taught you
to stand and fight, for justice. He gave your life a purpose.
And now . . . *(She is too overpowered to continue.)*

MAJOR

Yes? And now what? Treachery, as Hasan said? *(laughs).*
You are all little men. Like me. Our Leader, your husband
Alhaja, he was a great man. But his death taught you nothing. Nothing! When the man walking in front stumbles into
a pit, what should those behind do? Loyalty? Affection?
Love? Should they because of these passions follow him
into the pit? The grass-cutter of the forest, what must he
do to claim the elephant's legend? Dress himself in ivory
tusks? Listen, we were all brought up in the church and
what did you learn there apart from how to break the ten
commandments? There was a Messiah, once, and one was
enough! For all the centuries! One great monumental mistake and nobody since has been in any hurry to repeat it.
They crawl to the cross, they fall on their faces, wail and
moan, but no worshipper asks to mount it and leave his life
there. No! The nails and blood, the crown of thorns, all is
a charade, kept for the tourist value and the ritual of
house-cleaning. Afterwards are the buntings and the pic-
nics to affirm the reality of living, of survival. And it's
privilege, living. That's what the Leader's death says to us

if you will clean your ears! Every man for himself. And all the rest: 'rob the rich, feed the poor'. They're all part of the furniture. You hear! Each man for himself!

HASAN

You're filthy, Major. Your mind has grown rotten.

MAJOR

You can't understand? This is the end. The beginning. I am leaving the filth. I am leaving you.

HASAN

How long? How long will it last?

MAJOR

For ever.

HASAN

It will follow you, the filth.

MAJOR

This is money! Money! A new life. No more scurrying in the smell of back streets. A house the size of a palace! The law, tamed with my bank account! And children! Listen, I am going to be a daddy! I'll own the main streets, six, no, . . . ten Mercedes, the neon lights, the supermarkets . . .

(They try to rush at him, but he recovers instantly.)

HASAN

You're doomed. Major! One day, we'll come gunning for you.

MAJOR

I'll be waiting, at the Bar Beach.

ANGOLA

You won't be there to watch it, I swear! Nor will your children.

MAJOR

So you'll never learn? Angola, Hasan, Alhaja? The other side are winners.

ALHAJA

Only for a season.

MAJOR

For ever! We are of the race victims are made of! We dream, we hug the gutters till we're plastered with slime. Then we begin to believe that slime is the only reality. We build it into a cult . . . and others continue to lap the cream of the land.

ANGOLA

(edging towards him) You cannot escape. No act of betrayal will alter your kinship.

MAJOR

Stand back or I shoot! There is no kinship, I have crossed to other side of the street.

HASAN

But do you know the password?

MAJOR

I am going to fly.

HASAN

With what wings? What number of painted sports turn a sheep into a leopard?

MAJOR

There's no way of convincing you. I knew. That's why I am going away. If we meet again —

HASAN

Wait, Major. The Aafa gave us three chances. This is only the second.

MAJOR

I have enough. And only fools wait for a third time when they have all they want. There's no sliding back into slime for me. Only, if you like, I shall teach you my own part of the formula. But tomorrow, after I have hidden the money.

(He begins to back away from them, still having them covered with the gun. Suddenly, the noise of gunshots from his rear. He wheels round, only to crumble as he is hit.)

HASAN

The Soldiers! The soldiers, they're coming back!
(He runs, to try and help Major, but driven back by a salvo of shots.)

ANGOLA

Leave him, he's dead!

54

HASAN

And the money?

ANGOLA

Are you mad? Come!

(They run out just as the Sergeant bursts in with his men. One of them is wounded.)

CORPORAL

They're gone! They've run away!

SERGEANT

Too bad. We got only one of them. Recover that gun.

SOLDIER

(doing so, discover money) Look Serg!

SERGEANT

What?

SOLDIER

The money, it's all here!

SERGEANT

(knocking him down) Shut up, you fool! Can't you restrain yourself? *(Looks round rapidly)* Couple, take care of the money. And listen, you dogs who may have been cursed to eternal poverty! As far as we know, the robbers ran away with the money! Is that clear? We found nothing. Okay? Let us meet later tonight, at my brother's house. And if I catch anybody with a running mouth . . .

(He is still addressing them as lights fade out, fast)
END OF PART TWO)

PART THREE

(Same situation, some days later. Dawn again, almost as in PART ONE. Some soldiers are seen putting together a platform and a drum for what looks like an execution block, centre-stage, among the stalls. The job is nearing completion when the lights come up. One or two of the soldiers have their shirt off, but will gradually wear them again in course of the play. The text below is not rigid and should encourage free improvisation.)

SOLDIER 1

Ah this country self! If it doesn't reach the very last minute, nobody asks you to do anything: They must wait for the last minute, and then it's 'do this, do that! And I want the work completed before I blink my eye!'

SOLDIER 2

Na religion, you don't know? We have an abounding faith in miracles, ask any of the flourishing apostles on the beach.

SOLDIER 1

Yes, miracles, as long as there are underdogs like me and you to make them happen, Ah, I am tired!

SOLDIER 3

Some of us are born to take orders, you fool, so shut up!

SOLDIER 1

Not me. I am going to be officer, you watch.

SOLDIER 3

And you complain about miracles! Do you think it's the number of craw-craw on your body that they count for promotion?

SOLDIER 1

I pity people like you, you'll always be an underdog.

SOLDIER 3

Go on complaining like that. Then we'll see who will remain a bloody recruit, till retirement.

SOLDIER 2

Retirement! He's got to be a privileged recruit!

SOLDIER 1

Well, I am tired of these last-minute orders. I can just picture the Sergeant calling his wife one day: 'Darring! . . Answer! now.

SOLDIER 2

'Yessaaah!'

SOLIDER 1

'Darrring mi!'

SOLDIER 2

'Yes, di'yah! I'm here'

SOLDIER 1

'How many pickin we get?'

SOLDIER 2

'Pardon?'

SOLDIER 1

'Pickin, we pickin. How many we get now?'

SOLDIER 2

'Hm, which kin' question be that? Why you dey axe me? You know say na two I born'.

SOLDIER 1

'Na this tax form here. E say that if we get three children, we go qualify for rebate'.

SOLDIER 2

'I no tell you before? You see yourself now!'

SOLDIER 1

'Shurrup! By this time tomorrow, you hear?

SOLDIER 2

'Hen-hen?'

SOLDIER 1

'By this time tomorrow, I order you to born another pick-in!' *(They laugh.)* Believe me, it's no laughing matter! This platform we are just building for the execution this morning, suffering in the cold, tell me, how many days now since the sentence was passed on the armed robber?

SOLDIER 3

Seven. Eight self!

SOLDIER 1

You see?

SOLDIER 2

It was the contractor who failed to complete the job.

SOLDIER 3

Contractor? To build a platform for execution?

SOLDIER 2

Yes, I heard the Sergeant mention it.

SOLDIER 1

Tchei, this country!

SOLDIER 2

Contractor now, he went and bought Obokun* —

SOLDIER 3

For the Baba ke!

SOLDIER 2

And took a new wife.

SOLDIER 1

With government money!

SOLDIER 2

No, he borrowed it from you.

SOLDIER 1

I hope they punish him.

---
* Obokun: Yoruba name for a Mercedes Car

SOLDIER 2

Keep hoping. You think the contractor is a fool? That he spent the money all alone by himself?

SOLDIER 1

I see. So that's why we are suffering in the cold like this.

SOLDIER 3

At least you will have no complaint. It's still better than the guard-room.

SOLDIER 1

That's where your papa lives?

SOLDIER 3

If not for this job you think they would have let you out so soon? Insulting an officer -

SOLDIER 1

Officer na yeye *. I tell you, I am going to be officer too one day.

SOLDIER 3

By the grace of Soponno, god of craw-craw!

SOLDIER 1

Siddown there. I won't tell you what I am going to do first after the promotion.

SOLDIER 2

The worst you can do is to try and overthrow the government. And as for that —

---

* Yeye: rubbish, nonsense.

SOLDIER 1

Fool, how can I overthrow government when I'll be part of it? Let me tell you: all the fine fine palaces on Victoria Island and Ikoyi *, all the better lands at Ibadan, Kaduna, Pitakwa: ** and so on. I will declare them for government —

SOLDIER 3

Meaning, for yourself.

SOLDIER 1

With immediate effect!

SOLDIER 2

Thief man!

SOLDIER 1

Whetin. You never heard of African socialism?

SOLDIER 3

They will kill you one day, I assure you.

SOLIDER 1

And if their owners refuse, I inquiry them at once.

SOLDIER 2

And then?

SOLDIER 1

The Nigerians among them, I detain. The oyinbos and the koras —

* Victorial Island and Ikoyi: high class residential areas of Lagos.
** Pitakwa: Port Harcourt.

SOLDIER 3

You shoot them.

SOLDIER 1

Haba! Where's your sense of hospitality, or are you not an African.

SOLDIER 3

So what will you do with them?

SOLDIER 1

Bushman. With these oyinbos and koras, * the only decent thing to do is to form company with them. Import and Export Enterprises. Shipping Lines. Engineering Consultants (Nigeria) Limited, etc. For all contract above five million naira.

SOLDIER 3

Why that one?

SOLDIER 1

How many times I must tell you our people are too useless? Look around you. Which black man get initiative? No, my friend, anything big you must give to expatriates! Expressway fit for visiting Heads of State. Overhead bridges with shining posters. Docks reclaimed from swamp. Airports for concordes and discords. Hospitals, mortuaries, what more! Even self, if we elect Lady President one day, na white man go fit to fuck am . . .

---

*   oyinbos and koras: i.e. Whites and Asians

(Above their laughter comes the call of a woman hawking corn She enters, a covered basin on her head. It is Alhaja disguised.)*

ALHAJA

(calling) – Lagbe jino o!** Hot steaming corn! Eager bride for hungry stomachs! Eat my corn and kick like a thoroughbred! Langbe re o!***

SOLDIER 1

Woman, you're the answer to an unspoken prayer. We were just beginning to be hungry.

ALHAJA

I'm happy then, officer.

SOLDIER 1

(delighted by the appellation) Officer! Serve us, one naira worth! I hope your corn is as fine as you!

ALHAJA

(serving with a fork. They take it with their hands) Tasty, officer.

SOLDIER 1

(eating) Delightful! And are you as . . . as available?

ALHAJA

Depends.

---

* hawking corn: in production, other food items may be used, as convenient.
** Langbe jino: My corn's hot and ready!
*** Langbe re o: Here's corn!

SOLDIER 2

On what, I'm interested

ALHAJA

On how sharp your tooth is.

SOLDIER 3

Ah, you've lost! She wants me!

SOLDIER 1

She's not talking of wisdom teeth, you old rag. She means strength, like mine.

ALHAJA

Well, may be. *(Looking round)* Who's been building a platform?

SOLDIER 1

Me, of course. They were helping.

SOLDIER 3

You hear that!

ALHAJA

But what's it for? *(They look at her with suspicion. Hastily she adds)* There's more corn.

SOLDIER 1

(reassured) It's the execution. We get man to kill this morning.

ALHAJA

Ah, the armed robber!

SOLDIER 1

That's right.

ALHAJA

And you . . . you're the soldiers going to . . . to do it?

SOLDIER 2

Yes. It's our job.

ALHAJA

(Leaping on their necks in turn) Let me . . . let me hold you! Ah, I'm glad, so happy to meet you! What luck today! Take, eat more corn on my account! I never suspected that-oh, I'm so glad I don't know how to express it! Such courage! I mean, to stand and shoot a man, a dangerous robber! Not many men can do it!

SOLDIER 3

We are soldiers.

ALHAJA

How many soldiers can do it! I tell you, you are heroes!

SOLDIER 1

Well, well —

ALHAJA

Eat! Please eat more! At my expense. To think that — Ah, I too I am going to be a hero today! When I tell people that I actually met, actually spoke to, no, no that I even touched yeah! Touched the soldiers who'll carry out the execution . . .! I can imagine the envy! I'll strut, like this, watch me. I'll be like Emotan. Ah, I am going to become a legend! *(She dances.)* Please, eat and let me dance for you. . .! *(She dances and sings):*

Wo mi bi moti nredi - kenke!
Redi fun ololufe - kenke! *

(The soldiers, chewing, beat out the rhythm with their boots till their resistance breaking down before her overt sexual provocation, they join her. Finally at a calculated moment, she falls backwards, laughing, into their arms. As the move is unexpected, they stumble awkwardly forward and all fall down laughing).

ALHAJA

I just love you! You've made my day today! I will offer you something in return.
(She pulls out an ogogoro ** *bottle from the basin takes a swig and hands it out. The soldier are undecided).*

SOLDIER 1

See if no one's coming.

ALHAJA

It's not market day today, don't worry. People'll only be coming for the execution.

SOLDIER 2

You're right. It's safe

(The drink. She rises to inspect the platform).

---

*   wo mi bi mo ti nredi, etc. See me wiggle my waist for my lover.
**   Ogogoro: a home brewed gin

ALHAJA

Solid! That's why I love professionals. With the man tied up to this there won't be the slightest risk of mistake.

SOLDIER 1

Straight to the heart.

SOLDIER 2

The head.

SOLDIER 3

The kidney.

SOLDIER 1

We aim well.

ALHAJA

Good for them, these vermins. They pillage our homes, our offices, our markets.

SOLDIER 2

They rape women, pssshioo! *(hissing)*

SOLDIER 2

They steal children!

SOLDIER 1

They kill in cold blood.
(They pass the bottle more frequently now.)

ALHAJA

So wipe them out completely! Like this boy today! Ah when I used to know him —

68

SOLDIER 1

You knew him!

ALHAJA

Yes, unfortunately. He was not like this then. Edumare alone knows when he changed. For until quite recently, even until his arrest, every one spoke well of him. He was so gentle, so nice.

SOLDIER 3

True?

ALHAJA

Ask his neighbours. And if you knew his mama

SOLDIER 2

He has a mother?

ALHAJA

Not any more. She died in the war.

SOLDIER 2

Maybe that's what changed him.

ALHAJA

The mother was a . . . the paragon of virtue herself. It's said frequently that she has gone to paradise.

SOLDIER 3

It happens like that, alas. Good woman dey born bad pickins.

ALHAJA

She was almost a saint! went to church regularly. Taught Sunday school. She wanted to serve the country so much that when the war started, she-er, did you fight in the war?

SOLDIER 1

Of course! Right at the forefront!

SOLDIER 2

Decorated so many times that it became boring

ALHAJA

I guessed it! You must have met her then.

SOLDIER 2

Er...

ALHAJA

She wrote that all the officers knew her.

SOLDIER 1

Of course, I remembered her now! She was dark.

ALHAJA

No, very lightskinned!

SOLDIER 1

You're right! And kind of fat like this...

ALHAJA

Slim, so slim they called her Opelenge*

---

*   Opelenge: familiar Yoruba fondname for a very slim woman.

SOLDIER 1

That's the woman! Beautiful, with pele* marks on her cheek.

ALHAJA

Well, it's possible she got those cut at the war front. Anyway, to tell you the story, as soon as the war started, this brave woman, she volunteered straight as a nurse yes! leaving her own little boy behind in her mother's care and. .. and *(sobbing)* do you know what happend?

SOLDIERS

What ... happened?

ALHAJA

They were evacuating Aba, and there was this soldier, a little boy. Still in his teens, he'd already lost both legs. Moremi — that's her name, the mother of this so-called robber — Moremi ran back to carry the soldier, and ran straight into the line of fire ... and that was it, her son became an orphan.

SOLDIER 2

What a pity!

ALHAJA

Think of it! That boy she was trying to save, perhaps it was one of your friends! Perhaps she had even nursed one of you here in those terrible conditions which finally took her life.

---

* Pele: Facial beauty marks favoured by young girls and women, consisting of a short vertical line on each cheek.

SOLDIER 1

Of course there was that woman at Orlu, we never found out her name.

ALHAJA

It was Moremi! And now, her only son! See what they're doing to him.

SOLDIER 2

What they're doing to him?

ALHAJA

That's what the whole town is saying! Will you believe that? All because of Moremi, may her soul rest in peace. They say a mother like that cannot bear a son who will steal, that her son is being framed! They say he was in fact trying to arrest the robbers when he was caught, by mistake. That because the trial was so hurried, the jury never really hear his own side of the case.

SOLDIER 3

That's what they're saying?

ALHAJA

All over the town, I swear it to you! They say it's because he's poor and is an orphan.

SOLDIER 1

Just listen to that! I could have sworn the boy was innocent!

ALHAJA

They say the big guns behind these robbers are trying to shield themselves by framing this boy!

SOLDIER 1

Lailai! Is that what they're trying to do?

ALHAJA

You know how they're always using the poor against the poor! This boy now, he's just like you, poor, and an underling. So they get you to shoot him and nobody'll ever suspect them.

SOLDIER 2

Not this time! Ogun is listening. Not this time, they won't get away with this!

ALHAJA

You're not drinking. It's yours, go on. I met Kayode yesterday, Kayode Martins - you know, the football star, centre forward for the Cocoa Champion Club. He was in the company of his friends, on their way back from a match, and you know what they were saying? Very funny. That were they the soldiers guarding the poor boy, that they would not hesitate to release him — by mistake of course — allow him to escape accidentally from prison, but well . . . please drink, it's all for you . . .

SOLDIER 3

We're drinking, don't worry.

ALHAJA

Well, I said to Kayode, you don't know soldiers. When it comes to such things as upholding justice, they never interfere. Their ready excuse is always that it's politics, beyond their territory. They haven't the guts for that.

SOLDIER 1

What! You said that!

ALHAJA

I said — ah, look, here's Kayode himself, with a friend. *(Enter ANGOLA and HASAN)*. Kayode, you're not a bastard. We were just talking about you. You know, our conversation of yesterday.

HASAN

(hostile) Who're these soldiers?

ALHAJA

They're the ones going to —

SOLDIER 1

(coughing) Ahem, ahem! How're you Kayode?

HASAN

You're the ones going to carry out the execution this morning.

SOLDIER 2

Not really. That is. . . er. . .

HASAN

If you are, I want to meet you. Go and carry out your murder of that poor orphan, simply because he's not got money on his side. His mother, who died because of you, his mother will thank you from her grave!

ALHAJA

Kayode, don't be so harsh. You can't expect soldiers to be like football players who are used to acting according to their conscience. They've got to take orders, even if it's against someone they adore.

SOLDIER 1

No! Who tells you that! Who says we have no conscience!

ALHAJA

You can't help this boy to escape —

SOLDIER 1

Who says we can't! Who says we won't

ALHAJA

Look, officer, there's no need to brag. I know as soon as you return to the barracks, that'll be the end of it all!

SOLDIER 1

You'll see! Let's go men! The whole town will learn something today! And those big men who think they can frame an innocent boy and use the army to achieve their evil plan. Let's go!

ALHAJA

Officer, come back soon. *(Swings her waist suggestively).*

75

Your tooth, you said it can bite. I can hardly wait!

(The soldiers go out.)

HASAN

(laughing) Alhaja! You've not lost your touch!

ALHAJA

(smiling wearily) I'm glad it's over. I could do with some food myself. *(Takes out corn and eats.)* Help yourselves.

HASAN

(taking corn) You were marvellous! Just like in the old days.

ALHAJA

Thank you, Hasan.

HASAN

Like rabbits they scuttled off. They'll nibble off the prison locks to prove their honour.

ALHAJA

And Major will be free.

HASAN

Luck's always been on his side. He survived the gunshot, survived the hostile crowds at trial, and he'll survive the firing squad.

ALHAJA

Yes, luck's his mistress. The soldiers won't fail us. I know

HASAN

All we do now is wait.

ANGOLA

For his corpse.

HASAN

What?

ANGOLA

I said for his corpse. You 'really believe the soldiers will release him, don't you?

HASAN

They will, but if they don't, we know who to blame. But for you, we could have rescued him before now. We could have used the song Aafa gave us.

ANGOLA

And lose our last chance of getting funds? How shall we pay for those things we planned?

ALHAJA

The life of a companion, Angola, is worth all the riches of this world.

ANGOLA

But the life of a traitor? What's that worth?

HASAN

Are we going over all that again?

ANGOLA

We shall be here, when they bring him trussed up. They'll walk him up that platform and shoot him like a dog. He'll get the death all traitors deserve. In a common market, among the smell of stale meat and rotten vegetables. He won't even make the Bar Beach.

ALHAJA

Tell me, what do you gain from such hatred!

ANGOLA

He foamed at the mouth! You saw it, he was going to shoot us! His eyes burned like embers. He had caught a mirage, but he leaned on it as one leans on something valuable. On this very spot. You heard his cry of exultation, his song of lust! And for material things, cars, houses, neon lights. A companion! He was no longer with us, he had crossed to the other side of the street.

ALHAJA

Yes, Angola. And that's why he's dearer to me.

ANGOLA

The lost sheep, eh? Don't tell me, I know the parable. And I know he'll be the first to scoff at it.

ALHAJA

What does that matter? He's still one of us.

ANGOLA

Delude yourself.

ALHAJA

My husband made him one of his heirs. Like you.

ANGOLA

And our Leader would have been the first to disinherit him! To have him wiped out.

ALHAJA

Then you never understood my husband. Nor why he brought you together.

ANGOLA

Well, tell me - why?

ALHAJA

If I had thought - Hasan, you're the one with words. You talk to him, I am weary.

ANGOLA

Major will be shot, like a dog.

HASAN

And afterwards?

ANGOLA

After what?

HASAN

After his death. Yours. Mine. After our death? After the next betrayal, the hammering of boards together for the state-approved slaughter? What will be left?

ANGOLA

I don't understand. . .

HASAN

You trade in death and danger - by government decree your life's the cheapest commodity in the market, and you don't understand! Listen to Alhaja, man! There'll be nothing after us, you hear, nothing but the empty stalls and their solidarity of suffering, the blood stains. . .

ALHAJA

The market waiting for new corpses, for my sons. . .

HASAN

We're doomed, my brother, and only our solidarity saves us. From the cutting of the cord, earth to earth. You know the myths! What else do they recount but the unending tales of the powerless against the strong. And it's a history of repeated defeat, oppression, of nothing changing. . .

ANGOLA

Alhaja. . .

ALHAJA

(slow, as she enters a trancelike state.) Nothing changing. . . Only my story starting anew. Like before, like always, like ever more. The man will come to me, and together we will share Obatala's apple once again. He will lure me with the same deceits, enter me in a soft moment, and in the nineth month my bastards will spill out again like shit. Oduduwa will be at hand to nurse them, beat them into shape. The shit will breathe the air, drink the moisture of rains, and Edumare will teach them how to use their feet. They will

rise then, go into the garden arm in arm, their feet in warm dust, to where, at the foot of the tree, Ogun is waiting in a gourd to be discovered. They will drink then, my children, the sun will be in their eyes, the sun and Esu Laaroye, in all the cells of their brain, and one will stab the other and wash his hair in the blood. Then he will raise his head. Crowned with blood and freedom, and he will have won the right to give command. Plus, alas, the right also to die. And all who will not obey him will be scorched with the grass in the right season. Including me, his mother, in my withering. I will shout, I will call my husband. But lost in the stream of being, Orunmila will not respond. And all alone I will swell with the terrible burden of unwanted seed, unwanted because condemned to die. I will swell, I will explode, bearing the laughter of new corpses. . . *(She is sobbing gently still possessed. Hasan goes to shake her violently, but in vain.)*

HASAN

Alhaja! Alhaja! We're still here! *(to Angola)* See what you have done?

ANGOLA

Throw some sand on her.

HASAN

(doing so) Wake up! It's still morning!

ALHAJA

*(starting)*Where. . . where was I?

HASAN

Too far. Too far back. don't try it again, it's dangerous.

ALHAJA

It's always good to meet the gods again, but you're right. I'll pull myself together. Angola, I know how you feel, but we must learn to forgive. Those who fight for justice must first start in love and generosity.

ANGOLA

(stubbornly) No, not for those who have changed into monsters.

ALHAJA

You'll not relent? You—

HASAN

Alhaja, look! *(Points in the direction of town. Some sound, but still faint.)*

ALHAJA

(looks) Sango-o! Is my husband asleep in the grave?

ANGOLA

I told you, didn't I?

ALHAJA

(Passionately) Angola, listen to me before they bring him in. It's his only chance!

ANGOLA

He doesn't deserve it. I'm sorry, Alhaja.

ALHAJA

I hate you! Don't ever talk to me again. I don't ever want to see you!.

ANGOLA

Goodbye. *(Exits, sulking.)*

HASAN

Quick, come Alhaja. Let's get out of the way! *(They draw quickly aside. The noise increases, discernably now of voices and feet. Soon the crowd burst in, jeering at Major and the soldiers we saw at the beginning of the scene, but now stripped of their uniforms and also in chains. They are led forward by the Sergeant, the Corporal and other soldiers. The procession stops at the platform.)*

SERGEANT

Corple!

CORPORAL

Sir!

SERGEANT

As there is space for only one person at a time, you'll take them in this order: the robber first, then these sabos * in order of height! Clear?

CORPORAL

Clear, Sir! Soldiers get going!

(Major is led up into position, the crowd still jeering).

---

*   Sabos: shortened form of 'saboteurs'

SERGEANT

Prisoner! (Silence everywhere now.) Prisoner, this is your last chance. Do you still refuse the priest?

MAJOR

I've said it, Serg, I want no odours around me.

(General reactions)

SERGEANT

Is there anything else you'd like to say?

MAJOR

Yes. *(Pause. Deathly silence.)* This day is beautiful in the sunlight.

SERGEANT

Is that all?

MAJOR

Yes. The day is beautiful. Your stomach proves it *(laughter)* But man is so fragile, so easy to kill. Especially if he robs and lies, if he wantonly breaks the law. Serg, today that law is on the side of those who have, and in abundance, who are fed and bulging, who can afford several concubines. But tomorrow, that law will change. The poor will seize it and twist its neck. The starving will smash the gates of the supermarkets, the homeless will no longer yield in fear to your bulldozers. And your children, yes, your dainty, little children will be here where I stand now, on the firing block. . .

(Angry reactions.)

SERGEANT
Enough! You'll not repent, I see. Company, take position!

(They fall one knee.)

SERGEANT
Aim!

ALHAJA
Hasan, they're going to kill him!

MAJOR
Enough, you say?

SERGEANT
(counting) Five. . .

MAJOR
Tomorrow don't forget!

SERGEANT
Four. . .

MAJOR
And the day will still be —

SERGEANT
Three. . .

MAJOR

Like this, beautiful in sunlight.

SERGEANT

Two. . .

(Suddenly Alhaja runs forward and falls at the feet of Major.)

ALHAJA

No! Don't kill him!

SERGEANT

What the — ?

SOLDIER 1

That's she, Serg! That's the woman!

HASAN

(coming forward) Alhaja!

ALHAJA

I'm sorry, Hasan.

SOLDIER 2

Yes that's the other one! They're all in it together!

BINTU

You mean they're all robbers!

MAMA UYI

I recognize that one. He took my wallet.

MAMA TOUN

Yes, that woman led them.

CROWD

Shoot them! Kill them! Don't let them escape!

HASAN

You hear them, Sergeant: What are you waiting for?

SERGEANT

Hold your fire! They haven't even been tried! *(comes forward.)* Hasan?

HASAN

Don't touch me!

SERGEANT

Hasan! You in this gang too?

CROWD

Kill them! Shoot them!

SERGEANT

Stand back! Soldiers! *(They form a protective cordon round robbers.)*

MAMA ALICE

Give them to us, Baba Mayo! Let's settle our score.

SERGEANT

Mama Alice . . . I can't. Hasan. . .

MAMA ALICE

What?

SERGEANT

It's Hasan, my own brother

BINTU

Hasan! Let me see.

HASAN

Go away!

BINTU

It's me Bintu

HASAN

A corpse, like the rest

SERGEANT

But what happened, Hasan? Tell me.

HASAN

Same as happened to you. Washed up. You run with the hunters, I with the rabbit.

SERGEANT

When. . . how did you change?

HASAN

You tell me, Ahmed, how did you NOT change?

SERGEANT

I don't understand.

HASAN

Damn it, you understand! Of course you do! You're an animal, you're flesh, you're blood and urine, not a bloody uniform! Take it off! Take the damned thing off and reveal yourself, you smelling primate. Let's see if you're not skin like me. If we didn't come from the same womb. You eat and you belch and you sleep with women, you're a bloody human being. So don't answer me like a uniform. I said, you have eyes, you can see, you know what is going on everywhere, what is happening to people like us, so how can you remain unmoved?

SERGEANT

Who said I'm unmoved? I enlisted, didn't I?

HASAN

From one bloody corner to another, the world getting narrower, shrinking around us, just to give a few bastard more room to fart —

ALHAJA

Go on, Hasan! Tell him.

MAJOR

He enlisted. His stomach grows. As they fatten a sacrificial ram.

SERGEANT

Quiet! I signed off my life. I joined the victors.

ALHAJA

So keep running, beast of prey, among the hunting dogs.

SOLDIER 4

Serg, let's—

CROWD

Shoot them!

MAMA ALICE

No! Let's hear what they're saying!

SERGEANT

Hasan, you said, when you were leaving—

HASAN

Yes, Ahmed? What excuse do you think I owe you? Every one has his dream. Everyone has a point at which the dream cracks up. I have sworn never to be a slave in my own father's land. All I wanted was the right to work, but everywhere they only wanted slaves...

SERGEANT

You could have come to me.

HASAN

The family circuit, eh? Like a huge female breast eternally swollen with milk. But it's a mere fantasy isn't it? The family breast can be sucked dry, however succulent, it can shrivel up in a season of want. Listen, Ahmed. Teacher flogged us at the writing desk — remember his Tuesday specials, when he always came dressed in red — Reverend flogged us with divine curses at the pulpit, the light glinting on his mango cheeks like Christmas lanterns — and poor Mama, she laid it into us routinely behind the locked door, her work-hardened palm stinging even shaper than whips.

90

But for what? So that afterwards the grown man can crawl the street from month to month on his belly, begging for work, for a decent pay, for a roof, for a shelter from the pursuit of sirens? Ahmed, hide behind your bayomet, but I want to pay back all those lashes, and the lies, of teacher, priest and parent. The world is a market, we come to slaughter one another and sell the parts. . .

SERGEANT

It's not true! It can't —

HASAN

No? Ask these women. They'll chop each other to bits at the jingle of coins.

MAMA ALICE

(Angry) It's all right for your to talk. You stalk the street drunken, and idle, and strike at night. But we have got to feed our families, haven't we?

BINTU

We've got to pay the rent, pay the tax.

MAMA UYI

For the tax man has no friends.

YEDUNNI

And the headmaster wants his fees, threatens to send the children into the street.

MAMA ALICE

Brothers die and must be buried

BINTU

Sisters have their wedding day.

MAMA ALICE

Children fall ill, needing medicine.

MAMA TOUN

Needing food.

BINTU

And even the simplest clothes wear out and must be replaced.

MAMA ALICE

So who will pay the bill, if the market doesn't?

BINTU

Where shall we turn, if not to our stalls?

MAMA TOUN

How can we live, if profits lower or cease?

MAMA ALICE

How shall we survive, if the Price Control Officer refuses to be bribed?

SERGEANT

You hear that? You've been robbing from victims!

MAMA ALICE

The market is our sanctuary. *(The women sing the last verse of the song of the market.)*

HASAN

A slaughterhouse. Each hacking off the other's limbs. Kill quick, or be eaten.

CORPORAL

Serg, I now say this na your own brother. But duty is duty . . .

SERGEANT

You hear, Hasan? They're not with you.

HASAN

Do your duty, Sergeant. Today is pay day.

SERGEANT

We had a choice. You and your friends, my soldiers, and these traders. We could have stuck together and rebuilt our lives. But each went his own way and—

HASAN

I am ready to pay the price. But you?

SERGEANT

My mind is clear now. Soldiers, arrest them!

MAMA ALICE

Baba Mayo, It's your own—

SERGEANT

I did not choose it to be so, Mama Alice. Blood is an accident. It's only our beliefs that bind us together, or rip us apart. Hasan and I are on opposite sides of the street. All I can do is hope that he has a decent trial. Now to get

back to our work—
*(Breaking in suddenly, the voice of Angola, chanting the for-
mula.)*

HASAN

Listen!

ANGOLA

(As he comes into view:)

Adisuuru-gbeje!
Atewo-ni-yagayaga-fi-gboore!
A kii moruko iku ko pani lomode:
Apanisigbomode la a peku!
Odaramogbo la a le koto oku:
Apeja-pada-lona-orun-alakeji!

*(Confused with this unexpected phenomenon, the Sergeant
has paused, puzzled. Profiting from his apparent bewilder-
ment, the other robbers hasten to complete the entire formula:)*

HASAN

Olasunlola loruko a a p'Aje
Olasunloro laa p'Esu Odara
Ojinikutukutu-bomi-oro-boju:
A kii modi f'afefe ko ma lee lo!
A kii gbofin ile de era . . .!

MAJOR

Ire lo niki e ba mi re
Iyo ope lo ni ki e maa yo mo mi
Adunkan-adunkan ni ti kukundunkun!

ALHAJA

Bi iwin bi iwin nii soloya
Bii were bii were nii selesu
Ajotapa ajopooyi nii sonisango!

(The Sergeant has been turning in complete stupefaction to each speaker in turn. Now, too late, he realizes what is happening.)

SERGEANT

Zero! Fi . . .

ROBBERS

(cutting in urgently:) E ma jo-oo! Dance! Raise your voices in song!

(The stage vibrates with the clashing orders of soldiers and robbers. In that confusion, everything suddenly comes to a freeze. The lighting is intense. Then, from the auditorium, AAFA speaks into the silence, as he walks in for the EPILOGUE:)

95

EPILOGUE

(Walking round the auditorium) A stalemate? How can I
end my story on a stalemate? If we sit on the fence, life is
bound to pass us by, on both sides. No, I need your help.
One side is bound to win in the end. The robbers, or the
soldiers, who are acting on your behalf. So you've got to
decide and resolve the issue. Which shall it be? Who wins?
Yes, Madam? Your reasons please? And you, gentleman?
Should the robbers be shot? Please do not be afraid to
voice your opinion, we want this play to end. Okay, I'll
take five opinions, and then we'll let the majority carry the
day . . . yes?

*(He collects the views, making sure there is a full discussion,
not just a gimmick, and then, just in case the house decides
for the robbers, he says:)*

Ladies and gentlemen, the robbers win!

*(The robbers come out of their freeze and sing their song.
Hasan frees Major. The robbers rob the dancers, stripping
them of shirts, bubas, geles, even trousers. Alhaja fondles the
Sergeant's stomach. Then the robbers start on the audience .
. . who hurriedly begin to leave, as lights rise in the
auditorium.)*

*(But in case the audience decides against the robbers, then
the end is different. The robbers are all seized and tied up, in
a scene of pantomine as in the PROLOGUE. Major, at the
stake is blindfolded. Meanwhile the lights slowly fade to*

dawn light, as martial music begins. All the movement must be jerky, like in puppetry. The order is given, and the execution done. Major is untied and placed aside. Then Alhaja is led to the platform and tied up. The soldiers take position to fire. The martial tune rises to an intolerable pitch, and then abruptly cuts off exactly at the same moment as the lights are blacked out. END)

GLOSSARY

For the sake of productions for non-Yoruba audiences, the songs, incantations, etc. may need to be translated into the language of the new locale. To facilitate such a transference, I have thought it helpful to provide the following approximate renderings in English of some of the songs. I hope directors trying their hands at this play will realize however that there is nothing rigid in this. Dirges, for instance, normally possess their own specificity and, like proverbs or saws, never really translate well: so that, in fact, they should be wisely substituted for rather than translated. It is in this respect that the 'translations' provided here should be taken as guides rather than fixed requirements.

1. 'Iton mi dori o dori, etc'

An ancient tale I will tell you
Tale ancient and modern
A tale of four armed robbers
Dangerous highwaymen
Freebooters, source of tears
Like kites, eaters of accursed sacrifice
Visitors who leave the house desolate
Dispatchers of lives to heaven

A ancient tale and modern
A tale of four armed robbers
The day government fire burnt them
And the gang leader was caught
And his back was turned to the sea:

Death of the wretched, penalty of pain!
Yes he was condemned to die
To die brutally by bullets
Bullets of the rattling gun
Ha! man dies the death of goats
And so to heaven by force!

My tale is about four robbers
Who came to meet me one day
One day, as days pass away,
And said: 'Aafa of billowing robes!
Billowing billowing robes!
Billowing billowing mat
Billowing billowing beard
Billowing billowing wisdom!

'Ah please save us from them
From these your modern men
Money-making has made them mad
Money, empty money
Money-hunting, evil-doing
Evil-doing to amass property
Buildings upon buildings
Wife-stealers, marriage-wreclers
Who teach by the hard way of pain!'
A modern tale I will tell you
A tale of four armed robbers

Dangerous highwaymen
Freebooters, source of tears
Like kites, eaters of accursed food
Visitors who leave the host in ruin
Dispatchers to unexpected heaven . . .

2. *'Eni lo sorun, etc . . .'*

The traveller to heaven
never returns,
Alani, goodbye, till we meet over there!
The journey to heaven
is a one-way route,
Alani, goodbye, till we meet in dream
Whatever is food in heaven
You will share
You will not eat worms
Or centipedes
Alani, so fondly remembered . . .

3. *'Awa ti wa, etc . . .'*

We are what we are
and no apologies!
We are what we are, gate crashers
Who, uninvited, bash into parties

Consume the drinks
Devour the food
And loot the store
We're scapel-sharp, we're pungent
Ah do not provoke
For our gash is deadly
Our knives are long
And needle-tipped
Our wounds are ghastly, ghastly
We have no equals!

4. 'Bi e ba gbo giri, etc . . .'

If you hear the earth rumble,
quick, run for it:
We're those who make the earth tremble and
tear apart!
If you hear the earth quake,
don't wait at all!
We're those who make the earth quake and
split open!

5. 'O se kere-e-e-e, etc . . .'

It is nothing but overdaring
Nothing but overdaring
For the old hag who pines and pines
To be like the 'ora' bird
The bird whose flight is so swift
That before she can turn away
She has knocked her head into an obstacle
And been deflected involuntarily
But if the woman insists
Doddering old hag who envies youth
And longs to be spritely
To be a coquette like 'ora' bird
Push her forward, catapult her
Into the circle and ask her
To display her credentials . . .
Not all maidens, we know
Have supple breasts . . .!
It is nothing but ambition
Nothing but overdaring
For an old hag to pine and pine

To be like the swift 'ora' bird . . .

6. 'O ja lori obi, etc . . .'

You fall from kolanut tree
You fall from kolanut tree
And fracture your thigh
So you have to crawl on your belly!
Who finds something astray
And does not seize it,
Who finds something lying by
And does not claim it
Must be stupid or insane
Must be dotard or deranged
Kerikeri! Kerikeri!
Where are you from that guards
Dare arrest you at night?
Stupid robbers only
Are killed by guards at night!
Yes, they call us robbers
But we're about our trade
Whoever the devil tempts
Should try to block our way:
He'll see his intestines gush out!
He'll watch his kidneys in open air!

7. 'Eyi lo ye ni, etc . . .'

This feat becomes a hero
Hen hun hen (Yes, yes, yes!)
Ogun is marching to war
Hen hun hen
Is armed with seven testicles

Hen hun hen
One is loaded with bullets
Hen hun hen
Two are filled with wine
Hen hun hen
And four are brimming with sperm!
Hen hun hen
Ogun! I pay respects!
Hen hun hen

8. 'Omo Enire, etc . . .'

This 'incantation' is adapted from Wande Abimbola's record-
ings of one of the principal Odu of Ifa, on pages 63 to 65 of his
Sixteen Great Poems of Ifa, published by UNESCO. The trans-
lation here is different from his partly for reasons of drama-
turgy:)

Son of Enire
Son of Enire
Of those who strike sudden and sharp
Ifa, we invite you home!
Ewi of Ado
Onsa of Deta
Erinmi of Owo
Ifa, we beckon you here!
Gbolajokooo, who seats wealth
On sedate throne,
Offspring of elephant
With ivory trumpets
Ifa, hearken to our call!
Source of graceful palmfronds
Which dance and hum by the river

Ifa, we invite you home!
Shoot of tender palmfronds
So fresh and frail and young,
Offspring of two snakes
Which slide so fast on trees
Offspring of bush fire
Which spares the oorun branches
You offspring of bush fire
Which skirts the heart of forest
Ifa, hearken to our call!

9. Interlude: 'Iton mi dori o dori, etc .

I am still telling my tale
The tale of four armed robbers
Who came to meet me one day
Whom I gave a power to magic
The magical power of song
The mystery of song, force of dance
which will send hearers to sleep
I, Aafa, with billowing robes
Billowing billowing robes
Billowing billowing mat
Billowing billowng beard
Billowing billowing wisdom!

Yes, I gave them the right reply
To this your modern world
Money-grabbing has made you mad
Money, empty money
Money-hunting, evil-doing
Evil-doing to amass property
Buildings upon buildings

Wife-stealing, home-destroying
Teaching by the hard way of pain
A Modern tale I will tell you
A tale of four armed robbers
Dangerous highwaymen
Freebooters, source of tears
Like kites, eater of accursed meals
Visitors who leave the house in wreck
Disptchers to the heaven of slumber . . .

10. 'Eni maye je, etc . . .'

The man who relishes life
Will not try to climb a coconut tree
The man who loves to live long
Will surely not climb a coconut tree!
When the throat itches,
prepare for a cough,
If the throat scratches,
watch out for phelgm!
And if you host a Moslem,
You'll have to bear how many 'salaam-ailekun'!
Alas! when a vulture alights on the rooftop
prepare for the costs of a coffin!

No! No evil thing will visit me,
For only illness can be cured,
with death it's too late!

11. 'Adisuurugbeje, etc . . .

(The incantations here are adapted from collections of 'ofo'
made by O.O. Olatunji for his 1970 thesis, Characteristics of

Yoruba Oral Poetry, for the University of Ibadan. The transla-
tions offered here are different from his for reasons mainly of
dramaturgy:)

ANGOLA

> *Who lurks in patience*
> *to collect a pledge!*
> *The yagayaga plant collects gifts*
> *with open palm*
> *When you name the name of death*
> *he pledges you long life*
> *Death! Your name is*
> *Apanisigbomogbe, I name you*
> *Death! Your home of corpses*
> *is called Odaramogbo!*
> *I call it roundly, to win*
> *my ransom from sudden death!*

HASAN

> *Honour sleeps in wealth*
> *is the name we call Aje*
> *Honour beds in affluence*
> *is the name of Esu Odara*
> *Mothers wash their face in wealth*
> *as they wake in the morning!*
> *Who can wall in the air*
> *that it does not escape?*
> *Oh, how deep the ditch*
> *that will halt the ant?*

MAJOR

Ire plant has ordered our friendship
The male palm flower orders rejoicing
Eternal sweetness is the lot of sweet potatoes!

ALHAJA

At the sound of dance, the Oya worshipper runs amock
The Esu worshipper, at the call of drum
turns into frantic lunatic
The Sango worshippers woons in a daze of whirling feet . . .

•••

END

Once Upon Four Robbers

Femi Osofisan

Professor Femi Osofisan is the current Head of the Department of Theatre Arts, University of Ibadan. He is a recipient of many literary awards including First WNBS Prize, Independence Anniversary Essay 1965, *City of Pennsylvania Bell Award for Artistic Performance* 1982, First ANA (Association of Nigerian Authors) Prize for Literature 1983, etc.

Osofisan is a member of many learned societies, among which are Nigerian Association of African and Comparative Literature (NAACL), Nigerian Association of Literary Critics; President, Association of Nigerian Authors (ANA) 1988-90. He has published several scholarly works in literature. These include, *Red is the Freedom Road* (1968), *A Restless Run of Locusts* (1975), *Kolera Kolej* (1975), *The Charttering and the Song* (1976), *Morountodun* (1976), *No More the Wasted Bread* (1982), *Farewell to A Cannibal Rage* (1986), *Midnight Hotel* (1986), *Oriki of A Grasssshopper* (1987), *Minted Coins* (poetry 1968), *Aringindin and the Nightwatchmen* (1991), *Who is Afraid of Solarin?* (1991), etc.

He is married to Dr. Nike Osofisan, and they have four children.

OTHER HEINEMANN FRONTLINERS